THERE'S A HAMSTER IN THE FAST LANE

Brian Moses lives in a small Sussex village with his wife, his two daughters and several bad-tempered chickens. He writes and edits poetry and picture books for young people. In the past twenty years he has travelled extensively throughout the UK and abroad, presenting his poetry and percussion show in schools, libraries and at festivals.

Jan McCafferty lives in Chorlton, Manchester, with her teacher husband. She works from home, illustrating children's books and trying not to eat too much chocolate with her afternoon cup of tea. Before settling in the north-west, she lived in various places in the UK, including five years in London working as a designer at a publishing house.

Also available from Macmillan

Behind the Staffroom Door
The Very Best of Brian Moses

The Truth About Teachers
Poems by Brian Moses, Paul Cookson,
David Harmer and Roger Stevens

Taking Out the Tigers
Poems by Brian Moses

The Works 7
Classic Poems
Chosen by Brian Moses

The Secret Lives of Teachers
Poems chosen by Brian Moses

THERE'S A HAMSTER

IN THE FAST LANE

Poems chosen by Brian Moses
Illustrated by Jan McCafferty

MACMILLAN CHILDREN'S BOOKS

First published 2008 by Macmillan Children's Books
a division of Macmillan Publishers Limited
20 New Wharf Road, London N1 9RR
Basingstoke and Oxford
Associated companies throughout the world
www.panmacmillan.com

ISBN 978-0-330-44423-1

5 7 9 8 6 4

A CIP catalogue record for this book is available from
the British Library.

Printed and bound in Great Britain by Mackays of Chatham plc, Kent

Another one for my daughters,
Karen and Linette

CONTENTS

INTRODUCTION

'What pets have you got?'

This is one of the most frequently asked questions when I visit schools as a writer.

Well, at the moment my family has a semi-lop-eared rabbit called Miffy (one ear down, one ear up) and a loopy Labrador called Honey.

Honey arrived as a cute and cuddly puppy early in 2007 but has since grown into a gangly teenage dog that doesn't seem to understand what dog-training classes (or SATS for dogs) are all about. She's acquired a number of nicknames, including Honey Pie, The Honey Monster and Honey Houdini. Her favourite hobby is chasing rabbits, which she does joyously each day as we walk on the hills behind our house. She never catches any, because they run off in all directions and she gets totally confused about which one to follow!

And then there are our chickens: six wonderfully eccentric pea-brained creatures, the largest of which we call Boadicea, Warrior Chicken! There are also Twiggy, Darcy, Alice, Geraldine (or Vicar) and Letitia. (Anyone who's ever watched *The Vicar of Dibley* will know immediately where those last three names came from!) Ideally you should eat your chickens once they stop laying eggs, but we just couldn't do it! So Boadicea, Twiggy and Darcy have been pensioned off while still pecking up large amounts of food at our expense.

There were other pets in the past. Pie the springer spaniel regularly ate the contents of the kitchen waste-bin as well as his two daily tins of Happy Dog. Chum, my childhood dog, was a black mongrel who followed me everywhere. (When there was a storm outside he seemed to think that the only safe place for him was on top of the dining-room table, particularly if we were eating a meal at the time!) There have been a whole host of guinea pigs and their babies, fish of all shapes and colours, budgies, stick insects, newts and a tortoise that seemed to be permanently in training for some sort of tortoise marathon!

There are pets I wish I could have owned. These include a snake – python or anaconda (but my wife threatened to leave me if I got either!), a goat (so I could hand over lawnmowing duties), a Vietnamese pot-bellied pig (because they're so ugly they need all the friends they can get) and a turkey that I wanted to rescue from the farm down the lane a few days before Christmas.

I suppose, therefore, with all my experience of pets over the years, I am qualified to edit an anthology of pet poems, particularly as I also own a kung-fu, kick-boxing kangaroo (in my dreams).

The title poem, 'There's a Hamster in the Fast Lane', came to life when I read a news report about a hamster who actually did escape from a house where his owners had neglected to keep an eye on his activities. Obviously he had become quite skilful at moving around in his hamster ball and, when no one was looking, he headed for the door and freedom. The picture in the paper actually showed him disappearing down the road!

So now it's time to move on and meet the pets inside this book – cats, dogs, rabbits, frogs, pigeons, snakes, tortoises, oysters and socks. SOCKS?! How did they get in here?

Read on and find out . . .

Brian Moses

AlphaPet

Affectionate, boisterous canine

(dog) enjoys fetching,

going hunting, into junkfood,

kittycats, loves munching.

Needs obedient person quickly.

Requires stick throwing uphill,

vigorous walking, xercising.

                    Yours

                          Ziggy xxx

Celia Gentles

Ferret Fashions

There is actually a place called Ferret World, where ferret owners can purchase outfits for their furry little friends . . . here are a few more ideas.

Admire his style and watch him jive
Watch him duck and watch him dive
On the catwalk nine till five
The best-dressed A-list ferret

Parading all the latest styles
Beady eyes and razor smiles
Every night he's on the tiles
The best-dressed A-list ferret

Evening suit, cane, top hat
Monocle, bow tie and spats
Quite the cool aristocrat
The best-dressed A-list ferret

Burberry check, polka dots
Deckchair stripes, rainbow spots
He's the tops, he's the hot
Best-dressed A-list ferret

Leather jacket, baseball boots
Dyed his fur green to the roots
Pins and chains on all his suits
The best-dressed A-list ferret

Dressed for leisure – sleek and sporty
Dressed for pleasure – cheeky, naughty
Made to measure – that's his forte
The best-dressed A-list ferret

He'll pose nude without a care
Or in just his underwear
But one thing he won't wear is . . . fur
The A-list best-dressed beast on merit
Ferdinand the fashion ferret

Paul Cookson

Tortoise on a Trampoline

The bounciest thing I've ever seen
Is a tortoise on a trampoline
Turning turtle, fit to hurtle
Into space like a flying machine
Doing tuck jumps . . . demonstrating
Half twists . . . pike jumps . . . levitating
For a seat drop . . . belly flop . . .
Show's over, folks – he's hibernating!

Sue Cowling

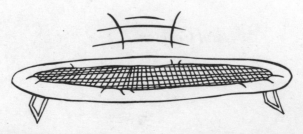

The Perfect Pet

Some think a tarant
ula's exotic,
it's not, it's
just something to make your parents frant
ic.

Forget
those fair-weather pets.
Slugs may be ug
ly but your snug
ly rabbit or hamster
(or even tarantula)
won't come out when it's wet.

Helen Dunmore

My Kung-fu, Kick-boxing Kangaroo

I really haven't a clue what to do,
should I sell him for money
or give him to the zoo,
my kung-fu, kick-boxing kangaroo?

He's king of the ring, a middleweight champ,
when he gets really stroppy, you'll hear him stamp,
if you say that he's great he'll light up like a lamp,
my kung-fu, kick-boxing kangaroo.

He's the coolest marsupial I ever knew,
he's the meanest fighter, but he's musical too,
plays electric guitar and the didgeridoo,
my kung-fu, kick-boxing kangaroo.

He thinks that lions are no big deal,
he's got muscles like melons and fists of steel,
you won't believe this but he's really real,
my kung-fu, kick-boxing kangaroo.

And I'd avoid him if I were you,
my kung-fu, kick-boxing kangaroo!

Brian Moses

Mirror Haiku

Look in the mirror

What do you see, pussycat?

I see a lion.

Roger Stevens

Hamster Tattle

My burrow's in the desert, I built its walls of sand
My cage sits in the kitchen, dear, designed by human hand

I scavenge all night long, and stuff my cheeks with grain and seeds
My bowl is always brimful of nutritious hamster feed

I run for miles beneath the moon, the wind ruffles my fur
I trundle in the jogging ball, a workout I prefer

I hibernate in winter, safe from desert storm
I don't need to hibernate; the kitchen's snug and warm

My water bottle's always full, while you have to make do
A water bottle? Who needs that? I sip the morning
  dew

My owner lets me out to have a little trot around
The whole desert's mine to roam, where bright night
  stars abound

Beverley Johnson

Cold Morning

Someone was sweeping a dusting of snow.

From the front door my dog appeared, suddenly,
her eyes fixed on mine, her tail a joyous flag
as she galloped and galloped to meet me.
I shrieked her name as she came
and held her gaze long enough
to feel her soft coat;
rub my head against hers;
sense her breath . . .
Then I woke.

Dreaming of snow's a good omen, they say.
And to dream of snow in autumn
foreshadows happiness . . .

I'd dream myself an avalanche
if it brought me back my dog.

Celia Warren

Losing it

Losing my chameleons

makes me lose my mind –

camouflaged chameleons

are very hard to find.

Jane Clarke

Song of a Cat Who Has Been Served the Wrong Brand of Cat Food in Error

I am not angry.
I am merely hurt –
Wounded by your cruelty,
Your cold insensitivity.
Did you think I would not guess?
Did you suppose I would not mind?
Did you hope I would not care?
See how my affronted nostrils shudder,

How my entire being recoils in disgust.
Is this how you repay my love?
How you betray my trust?
But I shall not protest.
I shall not drag my dignity through the dust.
I shall simply cleanse my fur with tainted breath,
And eloquently, elegantly,
Exquisitely,
Starve to death.

Clare Bevan

Breakout at Arkwright's Shop

Break out said the budgies, bust out barked the dogs
Find freedom now called the tree-creeping frogs.
Vamoose said the mice, the rats and the snakes
That's right said the cats, we've got what it takes.

The door slowly opened, Arkwright was back
He heard a slight squeak, he heard a faint crack
He suddenly was showered with cages and hutches
As the pets flooded out escaping his clutches.

When they got to the doorway they came to a stop
He cried out loud, 'You just love this shop
You need me too much, you can't run away
Now hop back and pop back, and do it today!'

They laughed at his words, looked under a shelf
Where a small cardboard box crawled along by itself.
You've got it all wrong he heard a dog shout
We're just making sure that the tortoise gets out.

David Harmer

Glow-worm Poem

Clare found this poem in the dusty cupboard where she keeps her torch.

My glow-worm glows
The whole night through –
It's what a glow-worm
Likes to do.
He lights my path
Between the trees,
And NEVER needs
New batteries.

Clare Bevan

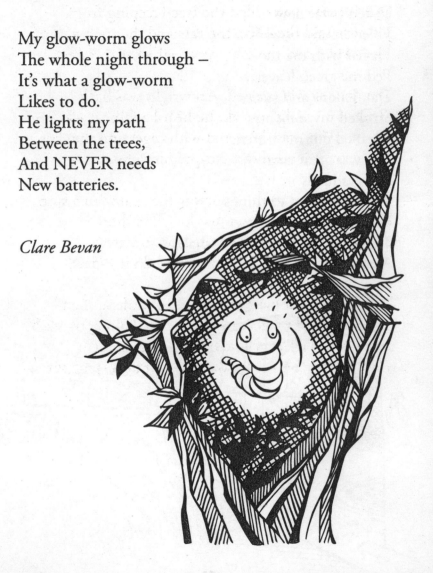

Sad Rabbit

How they fussed over me
When I was new:
Filled up my bowl –
Played with me too;
Fed me green leaves,
Dandelions and such,
Stroked my long ears,
Cleaned out my hutch.
Life was great then
But gradually
They found other things
And lost interest in me.
They had new bikes, a football,
A computer to use –

A sad, lonely rabbit
Was yesterday's news.
Now they don't even
Bother to come.
Who brings my food?
Not them, but their mum.
She says, 'It's *your* rabbit,
It's really not fair.
It needs a new home
And someone to care.'
So perhaps I'll be moving
To someone quite new
Who'll care for a rabbit –
What about you?

Eric Finney

Pet Food

The doggy ate his juicy meat

The budgie ate her seeds

The white mouse nibbled an apple

The rabbit chewed his weeds

The goldfish ate their fishy flakes

The hamster gnawed on a carrot

And by the smile on pussy's face

I think he ate the parrot.

Richard Caley

Walkies

Dog years tick tock tick quicker
than human years, they say,

so please excuse me if I pant
and take my time, today:

it's not my fault. I *ran*
before you walked or learnt to play.

By the time you started school,
I was turning slightly grey.

Blame nature and not me
if I'm past doggy middle age;

my book's nearing the end,
you're still on the second page.

Let me sniff a little longer,
shuffling through leaves –

autumn is my favourite time . . .
soon spring's blooms you'll breathe:

think of me, as you walk here, then,
our marvellous memories;

all that fun together, chasing,
running round these trees!

Yes, there's a reason why I'll pant
and take my time, today:

dog years tick tock tick quicker
than human years, they say.

Mike Johnson

Newt

It's better by far to own a newt
Than a bedbug or a bandicoot.
Truly, there's no substitute
For the ownership of a real-live newt.

I'll tell you this. If I'd a newt
I'd feed it fish and free-range fruit,
French food freshly fried en croute,
Baked-bean butties and boiled beetroot.

I'd dress my newt in a minute suit,
Shoving each claw in a wellington boot,
And every weekday he'd commute
To a management job at an institute.

In a war, my newt, as a raw recruit
Would learn to march and aim and shoot
And stand up straight and give a salute
And volunteer to execute
A daring raid by parachute.

And if life left me destitute,
My poverty utter and absolute . . .
Ah, well! I'd simply sell the brute
For a decent price cos he'd be a beaut.

And you getta lotta loot
You getta lotta loot
You getta lotta loot
For a newt that's cute.

Nick Toczek

The Menu at Hutch's

Something traditional...

Clover and nettle salad

Buttercup and daisy salad

Dandelion and couch grass salad

Moss and meadow grass salad

Something healthy...

Wembley turf salad

Wimbledon Centre Court salad

Bowling green salad

Croquet lawn salad

Something exotic . . .

Rush and eelgrass salad

Kentucky bluegrass salad

Italian ryegrass salad

Spicy Bengal grass salad

Something adventurous . . .

Motorway hard shoulder salad

Motorway central reservation salad

Railway embankment salad

Busy roundabout salad

Philip Waddell

A Poor Little Rich Dog

I'm dressed in very fashionable
little hats and coats
with a jewel-encrusted collar
round my mini, skinny throat.

My claws are clipped and polished,
my fur is tinted pink
and I travel in a handbag
lined with champagne mink.

My eyes are large and bulging
and I have a yappy bark
and now and then I watch
the big dogs running in the park

and I sit inside my handbag
feeling quite unnecessary,
just a tiny, pampered,
celebrity's accessory.

Marian Swinger

The Cat That Bites Back

For Judith

Sure, you rescued me
when I was a scruff,
so I ought to be grateful
and not play rough,

and you feed me tuna,
the finest brands,
but I still can't help it
if I nip your hands,

'cause I'm the cat,
the cat that bites back.

I'm more than feline,
I'm felion,
tough as cowhide,
strong as iron.

I call the shots,
I'm top of the heap,
when I want something
humans leap . . .

'cause I'm the cat,
the cat that bites back.

I'm the cat that bites
the hands that feed me,
but I'm not bothered,
I know you need me.

Your angry looks
are mixed with pity,
but I'll never be
your cuddly kitty . . .

'cause I'm the cat,
the cat that bites back.

I'm the cat,
the cat that bites back . . .

PURRRRROAR!

Brian Moses

Flash

Flash, the tortoise,
Is really a superhero pet.
You know the type . . .
Lightning fast, brave, courageous,
Muscles of steel, heroic and noble,
Ready to fend off evil at any given moment.

No one's ever seen him in his costume,
Which just goes to show how good he is.

Paul Cookson

Throwaway Pets

We were talking about our pets
And our teacher said
'I've got fifty-three pets.'

We all laughed.

He said 'Oh yes I have
Fifty-three of them and do you know,
Once I've got them, I throw them away.'

We all laughed some more.

The next day he turned up at school
With a basket full of racing pigeons
And he tipped them all out.

As they tumbled and jumped into the sky
In a cloud of soft, whirring feathers
Our teacher laughed.

'Don't look so sad,' he said
'They will all come home
Just watch them fly.'

And we stared and stared
Until each one
Was a small, grey blob in the sky.

David Harmer

The Flea That Fled

At a flea circus once in Bordeaux,
A pet flea performed feats like a pro,
   Till a big, bushy hound
    Passed close by and then found

It had suddenly *stolen the show*!

Robert Scotellaro

Dog Training

Doggone it! Who would think a boy would
  be so hard to train?
They say his breed's intelligent, but my
  boy has no brain.
I've tried to teach him doggy
  ways since I had
  him as a lad.
He's a loving, loyal
  friend, but he
  makes me
  barking mad.

When he was a baby, I thought he'd turn
  out right,
he crawled around upon all fours and often
  howled at night.
He gulped his food and slobbered.
  I was sure he couldn't fail,
but his teeth stayed blunt
  and stunted and he
  never grew a tail.

He doesn't beg, or lift his leg
against a tree or pole.
He drinks from taps and never
laps out of the toilet bowl.
He sits on chairs, he
sheds no hairs, he
doesn't chew his
wellies.
He goes on strolls, but
never rolls in
anything that's
smelly.

My boy isn't up to scratch. I
don't wish to be blamed.
I'm doggedly determined to get
him properly trained.
He's got to learn to change his
ways. He's broken every rule.
But I think I have the answer . . .
and that's Dog Training School!

Jane Clarke

Well-kept Secret

He lives inside my bedroom

My very special pet

I've had my skunk for five years now

And no one's noticed yet.

Paul Cookson

My Pet Oyster

I've got the greatest kind of pet,
It never seems to get upset,
Or bark or scratch or jump and fret.
   It's always waiting for me.

It doesn't get the rug all wet,
It doesn't eat me into debt,
Or make me take it to the vet.
   It really does adore me.

It never blocks the TV set,
It has the finest etiquette
And so, I say this with regret,
   The darn thing sure does bore me!

Robert Scotellaro

Sleeping Cats

Cats dedicate
their lives
to dozing,

stretched out
like pulled gum before
the gas fire,

parcelled up,
legs folded away
like stored tent poles,

tail tucked under,
slit eyes waiting to see
what happens next,

curled into doughnuts
on doorsteps, on
walls and window ledges,

drowsing alone,
too hot to purr
in smelted sunlight,

snoozing, half-awake,
murpling in ecstasy
on lazy laps

or lying heavy
as bags of cement
on warm beds

in the murk of night,
deeply asleep
for once.

Like Eskimos,
with all their words
for whiteness,

cats have dozens
of different ways
of sleeping.

Moira Andrew

Mother Doesn't Want a Dog

Mother doesn't want a dog.
Mother says they smell,
And never sit when you say sit,
Or even when you yell.
And when you come home late at night
And there is ice and snow,
You have to go back out because
The dumb dog has to go.

Mother doesn't want a dog.
Mother says they shed,
And always let the strangers in
And bark at friends instead,
And do disgraceful things on rugs,
And track mud on the floor,
And flop upon your bed at night
And snore their doggy snore.

Mother doesn't want a dog.
She's making a mistake.
Because, more than a dog, I think
She will not want this snake.

Judith Viorst

I Had a Pet Frog

Once I had a pet frog,
A pet frog green and warty,
He was the talk of the whole town,
The life of every party.

Whenever I took him for a walk,
The girls from near and far
All rushed out to kiss him,
My pet frog was a star.

I put him on my dad's chair,
So he could have a snooze,
And I nearly landed up in court
On a charge of frog abuse.

For my father, coming home from work
(And he's not a little man),
Promptly sat upon my frog,
Left him flat as a frying pan.

I gave him mouth to
    mouth,
I took him to the vet,
Who inflated him with a
    bicycle pump,
And that revived my pet.

I put him on the radiator
As it was ten below,
But his skin went try as the harmattan,
And his blood refused to flow.

I took him to the vet,
He soaked my frog in brine,
And after two weeks and three days,
My frog was doing fine.

Alas, my frog grew lonely,
Despite our special bond,
I introduced him to a lady frog,
Who lived in the village pond.

He visited her one Sunday,
A bouquet in his mouth,
But very soon he lost his way,
Turned north instead of south.

South led to the village pond,
North, to a busy road,
My frog was not familiar
With the Highway Code.

He did not look to left or right,
He did not wait to cross,
A milk float that was trundling by
Squashed froggy as it passed.

I took him to the vet,
Who prodded, pressed and poked,
Then shook his head and sadly said,
I'm afraid your frog just croaked.

Valerie Bloom

A Prize Exhibit

THIS SCATTY BOUNCER IS NOT
FOR BEGINNERS

Warning note on a cage in the rabbit tent
at the Hertfordshire County Show

I'm a flapper, a flouncer,
One of the winners,
But *This scatty bouncer*
Is not for beginners.

I've ears made for stroking
And a soft fur coat.
So you think they're joking?
Believe me, they're not.

If you're after a rabbit
That does as it's told
And, when you grab it,
Is easy to hold,

A bundle of fluff,
A cuddlesome pet,
Then you're not old enough
To handle me yet.

But if you're scatty
And a bouncer too
I'm the ready, steady
Rabbit for you.

So one for the money,
Two for the show,
Three for the bunny
And go, go, go!

John Mole

Poodle Peril

Hey meter man stand still!

Don't move a millimetre!

That poodle growling at you

is a meter reader eater.

Sharon Tregenza

Unwanted Gifts

I've got a pet cat
Who just can't seem to see
That dead birds and feathers
Aren't really for me.

She brings them so proudly,
And lovingly too,
As if she is saying,
'They're specially for you.'

I've tried saying, 'Naughty,'
I've tried saying, 'Shoo!'
I've tried sounding cross
But she hasn't a clue.

She just keeps on bringing them,
Day after day –
Why can't my pet cat
Understand what I say?

Clive Webster

Angel

When dad was a boy he kept a barn owl,
built her a cage at the bottom of the garden.
Don't want no dirty birds near the house
his mother told him,
specially not now with the babby an' all.
She were an angel said dad.
The owl, he grinned, *not the little un.*

Dad showed me a photograph.
Her face was a silver-white moon,
her feathers fans of pink sunset on snow,
the tips of her tail and wings
the mottled bark of branches.
She stared out from the top of a log,
talons sunk into furry brown moss.

Fed her on frozen cock-chicks said dad,
thawed them in the fridge,
freaked out me mam!
I wondered why Angel hadn't hunted,
caught mice for herself.
Couldn't let her out said dad,
she'd have escaped.
That made me sad.

She were bred in captivity, son,
never knew any different.
But I looked at her eyes brimming with blackness,
as if they'd taken all the light
and turned it into dark;
as if she'd once dreamed of freedom
and never quite forgotten.
An angel sent down to Earth
who felt the true weight of her wings.

Celia Gentles

Pet Giraffe

'I don't care if they laugh
As I walk my giraffe,'
Said Horacio Oliver Filtz –

Who would walk it each day,
In the very same way,
With a leash and a

l p

o a

o a

o a

o a

n i

g r   of stilts.

Robert Scotellaro

What's the Rush!

'Get up!'
'Get going!'
'Move over!'
'Move off!'

That's our family
bossing each other around
as our household wakes and shakes itself up.
While Harvey, our golden, olden Labrador
lies next to a flicker of comforting fire
and just . . .
yawns!

'Hurry up!'
'Hurry down!'
'You'll be late!'
'You'll be sorry!'

Shout father, sister, mother and brother
as we zip in and out of
bathroom, bedroom and any other room.
While Harvey, our golden, olden Labrador
brushes the bristles of woollen carpet with his tail
and just . . .
closes his eyes!

'How much longer?'
'How much more time?'
'Out of my way!'
'Out of the house!'

Doors, cupboards and mouths
fly open and crash shut
until we're all gone.
Except for Harvey, our golden, olden Labrador
who lazily twitches his rubbery, wet nose
and just . . .
welcomes sleep.

Ian Souter

Keith

I know an old tortoise named Keith
who takes two days to nibble a leaf.
Life moves pretty slow
when you've short legs below,
a shell on the back, and no teeth.

Rosie Kent

My Cat Has a Personal CD

My cat has a personal CD player.
A neat little compact device.
Wherever it came from I cannot be sure,
but I think it's a gift from the mice.

There must be a shop with one missing nearby,
and a hole where the mice come and go,
for there
on the cat's second birthday it stood,
by her basket,
tied up with a bow.

So why am I thinking the mice are to blame?
Well,
the reason I quickly discovered.
They scurry around without fear for they know
she can't hear them with both her ears covered.

Barry Buckingham

Mary Didn't Have a Little Lamb

No!

Mary had a little slug
its skin was tough and green
and when the slug refused to budge
oh gosh, was there a scene!

You should have heard our Mary yell
'I need you slug – for Show & Tell!
It's time for school – now come on, please!'
She even got down on her knees

But slug was not one to be swayed
and poor old Mary was dismayed
when slug set off and walked to school
all four miles – the crazy fool!

So how to end this oddly tale?
Did slug succeed, give up or fail?
Well, slug did make it to the gate
(of the school) some two years late

One half-term – so had to wait
till Monday morning – by the gate
but having come so very far
was flattened by a teacher's car

James Carter

Alice Anaconda

We are not really
into the pet thing
since the pet shop gave Alice
away . . .
    The pet man said Alice was loving,
    he said she just wanted to play.
But Alice ate grandma and grandad
and Alice ate great-auntie-Rose
she swallowed the dog and the budgie
and the bloke from the house down the road!
'Feed her each Easter,' said the pet man,
'Feed her on small things like mice,'
but Alice liked people
and puppies
and Alice was not very nice.

Peter Dixon

The Proper Care and Protection of Socks

Who doesn't feel tender
or heart-warmed at all,
seeing fluffy white socks
fast asleep in a ball?
We do take for granted
they'll always be there,
and then one goes missing
and causes despair.
A sock only survives
if it's kept with its mate –
you must reunite them,
take these steps and don't wait.
As soon as you notice
it's gone – advertise,
make posters, with photos,
showing colour and size.
Say when you last saw it –
give your email and phone,
though they rarely stray far –
most are hiding at home.
They're attached to their owners,
and we strongly advise,
give the run of the house
for they need exercise.
Problems? Some bite ankles
when small, though lacking in teeth,

and when aged some sadly
go bald underneath.
But they're worth any trouble,
as millions will tell – and
socks are NOT just for Christmas,
so look after them well!

Liz Brownlee

I Found My Dog's Diary!

Breakfast –
A *real* bone from Sunday lunch
Then to the park
With the boy
And the rope
And the poop scoop.
Met Dolores – my fiancée
The poodle from number two.
What a day!!
What a girl!!
She sniffed me
She chased me
She even outpaced me!!
Dribbled *all* the way
Home
In a
Daydream.

Chased my tail
Thirty-three times
In a row!
A new personal best
Lost control
Let one go in the hall
Still,
The boy's gran got the blame.

Keep itching my left leg
Hope it's not fleas
Off to basket now
Man-tired.

Daniel Laurence Phelps

Squeaker

My dad and me keep pigeons in the shed.
Ten we've got and most of them are grey,
but our favourite is a white one
and one day, at breakfast,
she laid an egg.

My dad cupped the egg in his hands
and we talked about what kind of squeaker
would hatch:

She'll be white, I said,
with wings like fire.
No, grey, he said, like me.
And we laughed about our squeaker
and put the egg back,
and we waited for weeks, to see.

My dad says he was a squeaker once,
bald and yellow and blind at birth.
He says he nearly didn't get out of *his* egg,
and yesterday, at breakfast,
he said it again.

My dad put the egg on the table
and we talked about what kind of squeaker
should have hatched:

She'd have been white, he said,
with wings like fire.
No, grey, I said, like you.
Then we prayed for our squeaker
and took the egg away,
and we cried, like we sometimes do.

Chris d'Lacey

A Proper Pet

You can stick your pretty pussycat,
Your cuddly puppy dog,
Your snooty prancing ponies!
How's about a squelchy frog?

A dear old croaky amphibian,
All slippery as the dew,
Wouldn't you like me to give you a kiss
As sloppy as frogspawn goo?

I could croak you to sleep each evening,
And croak you awake at dawn,
We could paddle and swim in the millpond
And leapfrog all over the lawn.

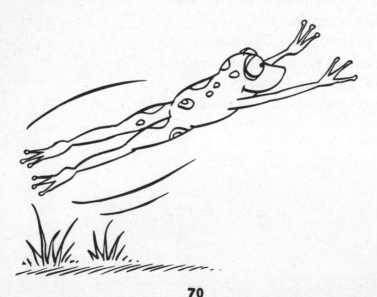

And, who knows, one day in the bathroom
As your teeth are getting a rinse,
You may see in the mirror behind you
A gorgeous handsome young prince!

Matt Simpson

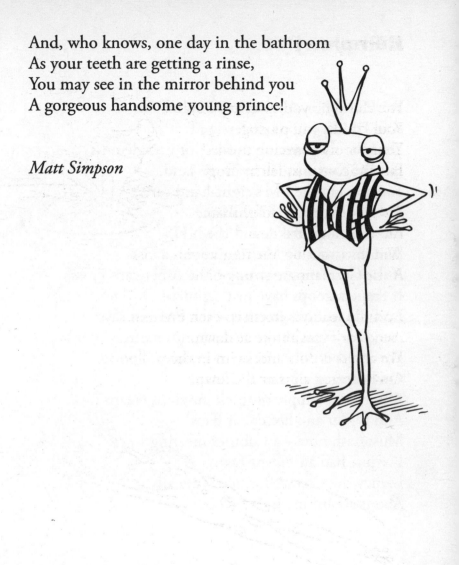

Humphrey

I'm Humphrey, the cat at Number Ten
And I'd like you to understand
That I'm no common mouser or fireside puss
But the foremost feline in the land.
You see, I'm the PM's right-hand cat,
The one he turns to for advice
On taxes and strikes and the NHS
And invasions by Martian mice.
If the Germans are stroppy, the Americans cross,
If French troops have just captured Dover,
And the world is in crisis – the PM just says,
'Send for Humphrey, he'll smooth matters over.'
I'm an expert on hijacks and crime,
On hostages, riots and kidnaps –
Also on the supply of thick, luscious cream
And bigger and better cat flaps.
Must dash now – a Cabinet meeting –
I've just had an urgent fax:
I fancy the Chancellor needs my advice
About abolishing income tax.

One last thought: I'm quite often asked,
'Humphrey, what do you actually *do*?'
And I answer, 'I work for a better world
For cats – and for people too.'

Eric Finney

Missing Monty

Based on a true story

Winter was coming
When Monty went missing
Oh, how I missed
His sibilant hissing

I searched high and low
I searched thin and long
Oh, where had my
Pet python gone?

Soon Christmas carols
Then Auld Lang Syne
Of missing Monty
There was no sign

Then just when I'd given him
Up for dead
On the first day of spring
He turned up in my bed

Safe in my mattress
Tucked away out of sight
Just think, I'd been keeping
Him warm every night.

Roger Stevens

Nine Lives of Sukie

There must have been more than two, the two
We can account for, unless we say your first was just
Too spectacular to merely count as one: that time
They found you, like a mechanic's rag, under the
      bonnet
Of a car someone had driven thirty miles.

And number two? The day you risked a dash
Across the street: that week in Intensive Care,
Broken jaw, loss of feeling in one leg.

Must have been others we never knew about,
Ear-tatterings on squawking nights behind dark
      hedges,
Mayhem among clattering bins down alleyways
      – forfeit-lives.

I can't believe that seven came simultaneously together
      here
In this small corner of our room, so quiet, subtle,
      catlike. It was
As if you were keeping an appointment. As ordinary
      as that.

There's profound silence now. Hardly a corner of the
    house
That didn't know you, which you didn't take as yours:
    wardrobes
Where pullovers pile, every windowsill, the patch of
    carpet by
The bathroom door your unfailing bum sussed out as
    where
Hot-water pipes ran underneath, and now I'm sadly at
    the window
Looking out at spots of garden that you knew the sun
    preferred.

Matt Simpson

There's a Hamster in the Fast Lane

The speed cameras are flashing
but they can't identify
a hamster in the fast lane
as he roly-polys by.

He doesn't show a number
and shades obscure his eyes.
Police reports all tell of some
boy racer in disguise.

For everyone who sees him
he's the cause of mirth and mayhem.
He's passing big fat four-wheel drives
by rolling underneath them.

No more tickles on the tummy,
no more crummy little cage.
One hundred miles an hour at least,
fuelled by hamster rage.

He's passing open tops,
he's passing executive cars.
His energy is endless,
no sleep till Zanzibar!

He's belting down the bypass
like a speed king on a track,
unsure of where he's going
but he knows he won't be back!

Brian Moses

Behind the STaff ROOM dooR

the very best of BRian MoseS

This brilliant book is packed with old friends – including 'What Teachers Wear in Bed', 'Aliens Stole My Underpants', 'Shopping Trolley' and 'Walking with My Iguana' – and introduces us to some wonderful new poems too.

From 'Aliens Stole My Underpants'

To understand the ways
of alien beings is hard,
and I've never worked it out
why they landed in my backyard.

And I've always wondered why
on their journey from the stars
these aliens stole my underpants
and took them back to Mars.

The TRUTH about TEACHERS

By Paul Cookson, David Harmer,
Brian Moses and Roger Stevens

Do you ever worry about what goes on inside your
teacher's head? Then these poems are for you!
Find out exactly what – if anything – makes
them tick (besides marking your homework).

IT'S A DEFINITE SIGN

Our dinner lady Mrs Mack

Is well in love with Mr Fipps

Because at every dinner-time

She winks and smiles when he's in line

And gives him extra chips.

Paul Cookson

A selected list of titles available from
Macmillan Children's Books

The prices shown below are correct at the time of going to press. However, Macmillan Publishers reserves the right to show new retail prices on covers, which may differ from those previously advertised.

Behind the Staffroom Door   978-0-230-01541-8   **£3.99**
The Very Best of Brian Moses

The Truth About Teachers   978-0-330-44723-2   **£4.99**
Brian Moses, Paul Cookson, David Harmer and Roger Stevens

Taking Out the Tigers   978-0-330-41797-6   **£3.99**
Poems by Brian Moses

The Works 7: Classic Poems   978-0-330-44424-8   **£6.99**
Chosen by Brian Moses

The Secret Lives of Teachers   978-0-330-43282-5   **£4.99**
Poems chosen by Brian Moses

All Pan Macmillan titles can be ordered from our website,
www.panmacmillan.com, or from your local bookshop and
are also available by post from:

Bookpost, PO Box 29, Douglas, Isle of Man IM99 1BQ
Credit cards accepted. For details:
Telephone: 01624 677237
Fax: 01624 670923
Email: bookshop@enterprise.net
www.bookpost.co.uk

Free postage and packing in the United Kingdom